SUMAYA SOLVES
THE WOODPECKER PROBLEM

BY AISHA AHMED
ILLUSTRATED BY HAMNAH RIZWAN

PICTURE WINDOW BOOKS
a capstone imprint

Published by Picture Window Books, an imprint of Capstone
1710 Roe Crest Drive, North Mankato, Minnesota 56003
capstonepub.com

Copyright © 2025 by Capstone. All rights reserved. No part of this publication may be reproduced in whole or in part, or stored in a retrieval system, or transmitted in any form or by any means, electronic, mechanical, photocopying, recording, or otherwise, without written permission of the publisher.

Library of Congress Cataloging-in-Publication Data is available on the Library of Congress website.

ISBN: 9780756587987 (hardcover)
ISBN: 9780756588069 (paperback)
ISBN: 9780756588052 (ebook PDF)

Summary: After watching a woodpecker pecking on a tree, Sumaya worries it could be hurting itself. She makes a plan to help protect the woodpecker.

Designer: Heidi Thompson

Cover artist: Loilufy

Any additional websites and resources referenced in this book are not maintained, authorized, or sponsored by Capstone. All product and company names are trademarks™ or registered® trademarks of their respective holders.

Printed and bound in the USA. 6121

TABLE OF CONTENTS

CHAPTER 1
WHAT'S THAT TAPPING?......7

CHAPTER 2
A WOODPECKER PLAN.......13

CHAPTER 3
SHARING HER PLAN........21

HI, I'M SUMAYA!

My family moved to the United States from Somalia, a country in East Africa. I am eight years old, and I am very curious about nature and the world around me.

MY FAMILY!

SOMALI GLOSSARY

aabo (AH-boh)—dad or father

haa (HAH)—yes

hooyo (HOO-yoh)—mom or mother

mahadsanid (mah-HAD-sah-nid)—thank you

CHAPTER 1
WHAT'S THAT TAPPING?

Tap, tap, tap, tap, tap.

One day, while exploring her backyard, Sumaya heard a tapping sound.

Tap, tap, tap, tap, tap.

Sumaya decided to investigate. She followed the taps until she spotted a woodpecker up in a tree. The bird was pecking at a spot on the tree's trunk.

Sumaya called her mother and father. "Hooyo! Aabo! Come quick!"

Sumaya's parents joined her beneath the tree. Her younger brother, Sahal, toddled along. He was curious too.

Sumaya pointed at the woodpecker. "Look at that bird!" she said. "Why is it pecking the tree?"

Her aabo answered, "That is a woodpecker, Sumaya. They peck trees to find food."

"Really?! They eat wood?!" Sumaya said, surprised.

Hooyo said, "Woodpeckers do not eat wood. They eat insects that live under the tree bark."

Sumaya giggled, imagining woodpeckers enjoying their bug food.

"Hooyo, are there woodpeckers in Somalia?" Sumaya asked.

"Haa," Hooyo said, nodding. "There are woodpeckers in Somalia and in many other parts of the world."

CHAPTER 2

A WOODPECKER PLAN

The family continued to watch the woodpecker peck away at the tree. But Sumaya started to worry.

If that woodpecker doesn't stop pecking soon, it might hurt its beak, she thought. *And what about its head?*

Sumaya decided that she was going to do something to help protect the woodpecker.

"I'll be inside," she told her parents. "I have a problem to solve."

Sumaya gathered a notebook and her colored pencils. She focused on the woodpecker's beak first.

What could I make for the woodpecker to help protect its beak? she wondered.

Metal was hard. Maybe she could cut out a piece of metal in the shape of a cone. Then she could place it over the woodpecker's beak.

She sketched out the bird's beak with a protective metal cone on it.

Next she focused on the woodpecker's head.

What could I make for the woodpecker to help protect its head? she asked herself.

When people ride bikes, they wear helmets to protect their heads. Maybe I could make that bird a little helmet, she thought.

Sumaya sketched out the woodpecker's head with a helmet on it.

Sumaya looked over her sketches. She was ready to share them with her family. Maybe they could help her make the beak cover and helmet.

CHAPTER 3
SHARING HER PLAN

"Hooyo! Aabo! Sahal!" Sumaya called. "Please come to the dining table. I have something to show you."

Sumaya held up her sketches. "I am worried about the woodpecker getting hurt. I want to help it by making something to protect its beak and head."

"This is a wonderful plan, Sumaya!" Aabo said.

"This is impressive, Sumaya! You made beautiful sketches. You are very talented," Hooyo said.

"Mahadsanid, Aabo. Thank you. Mahadsanid, Hooyo," Sumaya said.

"It is wonderful that you want to help the woodpecker, dear," said Aabo. "But do you know that woodpeckers have a special skull and neck muscles that protect their head while they peck?

"Their beaks are also designed in a special way so that they don't break when they peck on trees," he added.

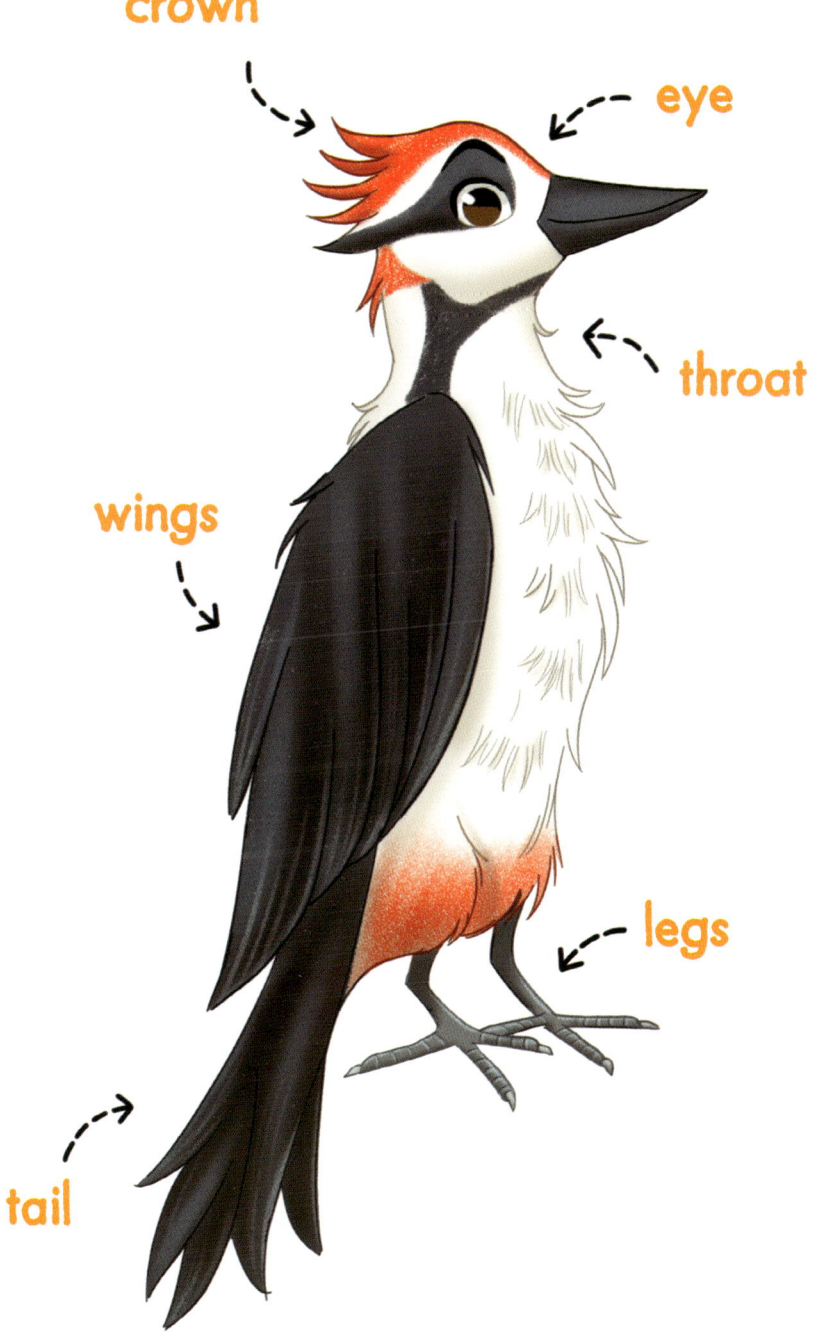

"That's amazing! I guess the woodpecker's body is designed to do the woodpecker's job," Sumaya said.

"That it is, Sumaya!" said Hooyo. "Nature's designs are often like that."

"I want to learn more about nature's designs!" Sumaya said.

Aabo smiled. "Stay curious, and you are sure to learn it all, Sumaya!"

SUMAYA SHARES MORE ABOUT WOODPECKERS

I loved learning about woodpeckers from my aabo. But I had more questions about woodpeckers and all their pecking. So I made a list of questions in my notebook. Then I went to the library to learn more.

Here is what I learned!

1. What kind of bugs do woodpeckers eat? Do they eat anything else?

Woodpeckers eat many kinds of insects including termites, spiders, ants, caterpillars, worms, and grubs. They also eat fruits, tree sap, small rodents, lizards, nuts, and bird eggs.

2. Does the pecking hurt the trees?

Woodpecker pecking does not hurt trees. It can help trees by removing insects and insect eggs that might make the trees sick.

3. Do woodpeckers ever tap on things other than trees?

Woodpeckers sometimes peck on houses, buildings, and fences in search of food.

4. We know that woodpeckers peck to find food. Are there any other reasons they peck?

Yes! Woodpeckers peck wood to make nests for their eggs, to mark their territory, and to communicate with other woodpeckers. They might also peck to attract a mate.

5. Do woodpeckers have any predators?

Woodpeckers have many predators including foxes, hawks, coyotes, and even bobcats.

GLOSSARY

curious (KYOOR-ee-uhs)—eager to explore and learn about new things

design (di-ZYN)—to make a plan for how to build something

impressive (im-PRES-iv)—having the power to gain interest or admiration

investigate (in-VESS-tuh-gate)—to search for facts to solve a problem or answer a question

protective (pruh-TEK-tiv)—having qualities that keeps something safe from injury

sketch (SKECH)—to make a quick, rough drawing; also a rough drawing

THINK ABOUT THE STORY

1. Why do woodpeckers peck wood?

2. Why was Sumaya worried about the woodpecker?

3. What did Sumaya want to do to help the woodpecker?

4. What did you learn about woodpeckers?

5. How do woodpeckers and trees help each other?

ABOUT THE AUTHOR

Aisha Ahmed is a Somali American author with a background in engineering. She was born in East Africa to Somali parents and immigrated to Minnesota as a teenager. Aisha enjoys being out in nature and learning more about the natural world. Aisha also writes stories for older readers.

ABOUT THE ILLUSTRATOR

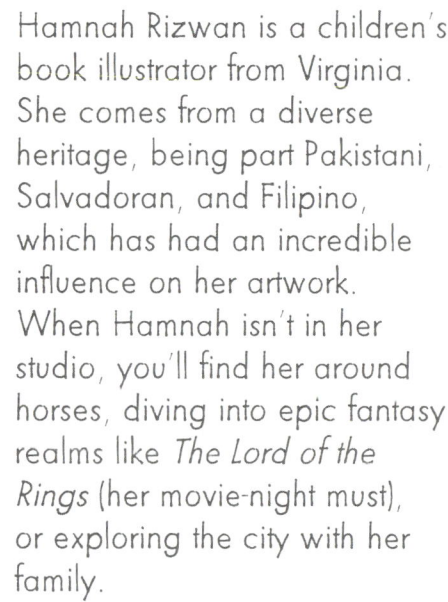

Hamnah Rizwan is a children's book illustrator from Virginia. She comes from a diverse heritage, being part Pakistani, Salvadoran, and Filipino, which has had an incredible influence on her artwork. When Hamnah isn't in her studio, you'll find her around horses, diving into epic fantasy realms like *The Lord of the Rings* (her movie-night must), or exploring the city with her family.